ABOMINABLE

DREAMWORKS

PEARL

MEET EVEREST!

Adapted by Tina Gallo
Illustrated by Mauricio Abril

Simon Spotlight
New York London Toronto Sydney New Delhi

SIMON SPOTLIGHT
An imprint of Simon & Schuster Children's Publishing Division
1230 Avenue of the Americas, New York, New York 10020
This Simon Spotlight paperback edition August 2019
© 2019 Universal Studios and Shanghai Pearl Studio Film and Television Technology Co.
All Rights Reserved.
All rights reserved, including the right of reproduction in whole or in part in any form.
SIMON SPOTLIGHT and colophon are registered trademarks of Simon & Schuster, Inc.
For information about special discounts for bulk purchases, please contact Simon &
Schuster Special Sales at 1-866-506-1949 or business@simonandschuster.com.
Manufactured in the United States of America 0719 LAK
2 4 6 8 10 9 7 5 3 1
ISBN 978-1-5344-4874-2
ISBN 978-1-5344-4875-9 (eBook)

This is a yeti.
His name is Everest.
How did he get such an interesting name?
Well, it's an interesting story!

Our story begins with an adorable yeti running loose in the streets of a busy city in China. He is lost, and isn't used to being in such a crowded place. He dodges cars and scooters and bikes.

He finally decides to hide at the top of a twelve-story apartment building. The yeti slumps on the roof. He is very tired and hungry.

While on the rooftop, the lonely yeti catch[es]
sight of a giant television screen. He can't st[op]
staring at the image on the monitor. He is loo[king]
at an image of Mount Everest. It is his home.

This is Yi. She lives with her mom and her grandmother. She has created a cozy fort on the roof of her apartment building where she goes to play her violin. When everyone is distracted or asleep, she sneaks up to her fort.

Yi loves to escape to her fort. It's her favorite place. She keeps postcards of places she will visit someday. Under a wilted orchid, she also keeps a secret stash of money that she's earned. It's money that she plans to use to travel across China.

Yi reaches behind some pillows and pulls out her violin case. She takes out her violin and begins to play. While she is playing, she notices a helicopter overhead. The people in the helicopter are looking for the yeti.

Yi is startled by the helicopter and drops her violin. Just then a furry paw reaches for it! Yi and the yeti see each other for the first time. He roars at Yi. She is very frightened. Suddenly the yeti moans. Yi notices a cut on his arm.

Yi realizes that whoever is in the helicopter is probably looking for the yeti.

Luckily, the helicopter doesn't spot either of them and leaves. The yeti is exhausted and falls asleep. Yi isn't afraid of him anymore. She falls asleep next to him.

When Yi awakens, she decides to help take care of the yeti's injured arm. She goes to the pharmacy to buy ointment and bandages for his cut. Then she goes back home. Her grandmother is making pork buns in the kitchen. Yi grabs a bunch of them for the yeti.

Yi brings the pork buns to the roof.
"Hey, are you hungry?" Yi calls out.
He certainly is. He reaches out with his furry paw and takes the whole pile! While he is eating, Yi bandages his wound. At first he snarls, but eventually he lets her help him.

When Yi tries to leave the roof again, the yeti is upset.
"Don't be scared," Yi says, and she plays her violin for him.
The yeti starts humming, and his fur pulses with a blue light.
While the yeti hums, the wilted orchid where Yi hides her money

Then the yeti spots the jumbo television screen again.
Yi sees him staring at the image of Mount Everest. "Do you know that place?" Yi asks. "Is that your home?" She makes a triangle with her fingers. "Home," she repeats.
The yeti coos and makes the same triangle with his fingers.

Just then Yi's friend Peng and his cousin Jin go to the roof and see Yi with the yeti. Jin gasps. He calls the police. Then Yi sees the helicopter overhead again, and is scared for her new friend.

"Go! Run! Now!" she tells the yeti.

He throws Yi on his back, and leaps off the building.

Yi and the yeti race toward the docks. Yi sees a cargo ship and
tells him to get on it. "Don't stop until you're home, okay?"
she says.

The yeti gets on the ship and hides behind a crate. He looks
worried and confused.

At the last minute, Yi decides to join him. She also decides to
name the yeti Everest! Everest lets out a happy hoot of relief.

Peng and Jin arrive at the ship. Peng is thrilled to jump aboard. Jin isn't so sure at first. When the ship arrives at its destination, they get off to explore.

They are all hungry. Everest begins to hum. His fur glows blue again. Then hundreds of huge blueberries appear on nearby bushes!

After a short rest, the group starts heading toward Mount Everest, even though it is thousands of miles away.

Just then they spot drones above them. The drones are following Everest!

As the drones close in, Everest makes a dandelion grow large enough to carry them away! Jin jumps but doesn't make it onto the magical dandelion in time.

Yi, Peng, and Everest escape! The magical dandelion safely lands in a desert.

The group walks for hours in the hot sun. They are tired and thirsty, and they stop to rest near a stream. They spot some koi fish swimming upstream.

"They're heading home," Yi says, giving the group the motivation to keep going.

They finally reach a fishing village and are reunited with Jin. They find a small boat.

The people who want to capture Everest are still after them. So Everest turns a field of beautiful flowers into a wave they can ride!

As Everest hums, the wave gets bigger and bigger. The huge wave causes the boat to capsize in an ocean of flowers.

The gang quickly recovers and manages to finally escape from the people trying to capture Everest. They are even more determined to get Everest back home.

Soon their journey to Mount Everest has ended. The yeti is home!

Yi, Peng, and Jin say goodbye to their good friend. They will never forget how they met a yeti they called Everest.